DAVID MORTIMORE BAXTER

Stranded!

by Karen Tayleur

illustrated by Brann Garvey

STONE ARCH BOOKS
www.stonearchbooks.com

David Mortimore Baxter is published by Stone Arch Books
151 Good Counsel Drive, P.O. Box 669
Mankato, Minnesota 56002
www.stonearchbooks.com

Library of Congress Cataloging-in-Publication Data
Tayleur, Karen.
  Stranded: David Mortimore Baxter Gets Trapped / by Karen Tayleur;
illustrated by Brann Garvey.
    p. cm. — (David Mortimore Baxter)
    ISBN 978-1-4342-1199-6 (library binding)
    [1. Snow—Fiction. 2. School field trips—Fiction. 3. Games—Fiction.]
I. Garvey, Brann, ill. II. Title.
PZ7.T21149St 2009
[Fic]—dc22   2008031681

Summary:
Snow Camp is supposed to be a week of skiing, snowboarding, hot chocolate, and
fun. But when a blizzard strikes, David and his classmates are stuck inside . . . with
no TV! They'll have to make their own fun by playing lots of games (and sharing
all of the rules!). The storm drags on, and the friends start to wonder if they'll ever
be able to leave Snow Camp or see their homes again!

Creative Director: Heather Kindseth
Graphic Designer: Carla Zetina-Yglesias

Photo Credits
Delaney Photography, cover

1 2 3 4 5 6 14 13 12 11 10 09

Printed in the United States of America

Table of Contents

CHAPTER 1

THE DON'T LIST

There are two things in the world that I live for — **weekends** and **holidays**. I think the idea of a weekend is **all wrong**. Two days just isn't enough time.

Long weekends are **GOOD**, because that means you get to have three days off from school instead of two. But by that third day, I can't stop thinking about how **TERRIBLE** it is that I have to go to school the next day.

That's why I was so happy about **Snow Camp**. We were getting four days off from school in a row to go skiing and snowboarding. **I hate being cold,** but **four days off** from school was going to be worth it.

Not that I was completely away from school. It was a school trip, after all. But a school trip is not at all the same as being at school.

For example, **Victor Sneddon**, our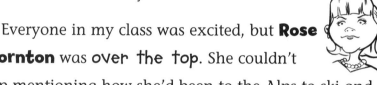
school bully, was not coming to camp.
The lunch lady, who loves to tell me
what to do, was not coming to camp. And Ms.
Stacey, our teacher, had promised that we'd have **no homework** for four days.

Everyone in my class was excited, but **Rose**
Thornton was over the top. She couldn't
stop mentioning how she'd been to the Alps to ski and
how she had her own skis and gear.

I didn't care about skiing, though. I wanted to
try snowboarding, which looked a lot like surfing
on snow. Not that I could surf on water, but hey,
how hard could it be?

As usual, **Ms. Stacey** had a list of dos
and don'ts (mostly don'ts) for Snow Camp.

My best friend, **Joe Pagnopolous**, wanted to
bring his portable DVD player. That was on the Don't
list.

"How am I going to survive four days without
a DVD?" he whined. **"It sounds like prison."**

My other best friend, **Bec Trigg**, wasn't
allowed to bring her pet rat, Ralph. The Don't
list said, "No pets."

I thought we should take the Secret Club Book —
or The Book, as we called it — so we checked out the
list. There wasn't anything on Ms. Stacey's Don't list
about bringing Secret Club Books, so Bec packed it in
her suitcase.

The **Secret Club** is actually a secret club, but we
hadn't come up with a real name yet. Its members
are Joe and Bec and me. The Secret Club has a secret
handshake, a secret call, a secret password, and secret
spy signals.

We hang around the park near my house and
practice our spy skills just in case we ever need to
spy on anyone. And we keep a notebook with all
of our notes from our meetings. That's The Book.

So the Secret Club — and the rest of our class at
school — was going to Snow Camp. I packed my bag
a couple of days before Snow Camp. I had to pack my
bag three times. The first time, I FORGOT to check
the packing checklist.

When Mom asked if I had packed an extra pair of shoes, I realized **I hadn't packed any shoes**. Or socks. Or underwear.

So I took everything out of my bag and packed again. Then **Mom** said she wanted to look at what I had packed, so I had to unpack again so she could check.

"Aren't you going to bring any board games?" she asked.

Electronic games were on the DON'T list.

I shook my head. "Too boring," I said. "Anyway, I'm going to be busy snowboarding."

"What about at night?" asked Mom.

"We'll probably just watch TV," I said. "Don't worry, Mom. I'm not going to have a chance to play board games. I probably won't even have time to sleep."

Then **Dad** suggested that I bring his ski gear.

"I didn't know you had ski gear," I said.

Dad laughed. "In my younger days you couldn't keep me away from the slopes," he said. "I was a real **Mogul Muncher**."

"A what?" I asked.

"A Mogul Muncher," said Dad. "You do know what a mogul is, don't you?"

"Ummm, sure," I said. "Mogul Muncher. Hey, you must have been really good, Dad."

"Well, I don't like to BRAG," Dad said, even though that was exactly what he was doing.

Then I had to follow him out to the garage to find his ski gear. Our garage is where all of our stuff goes that doesn't fit in the house. It just kind of gets shoved into the garage. Mom keeps talking about Dad cleaning out the garage one day, but it never happens.

It took us an hour before we found Dad's ski gear. It was a huge waste of time. Dad's skis were **really old**. They looked like two planks of wood with a space to slip your boot into.

"My CR Racers," he said, smoothing his hand along one ski. "Aren't they BEAUTIFUL?"

"They're sure something," I said, trying to sound nice. "Where's your snowboard?"

"Snowboard?" said Dad.

"I wasn't planning on skiing," I said. "I want to **snowboard**."

"Snowboard?" Dad asked. He scratched his head. "I've never used a snowboard. But here, try these boots on."

Dad's ski boots were **too big**. His coat sleeves were **too long**, and his goggles had **fallen apart** in their bag. The only things he had that I could use were his special ski gloves. Dad said they would keep me dry **no matter what**.

"Well, thanks, Dad," I said as we left the garage.

He seemed to be happy that I'd found something I could use, so I guess that was the main thing.

The day before we left for Snow Camp, **Ms. Stacey** gave us a huge talk.

She made a really big deal about how we should never go out into the snow without a **buddy**. She said we were never to leave the ski lodge or our cabin without telling someone first. And she said if we did happen to find ourselves lost, we had to stay put and wait to be RESCUED.

While she talked, I was too busy thinking that I would need to find out what a Mogul Muncher was and wondering whether I could fit some snack food into my bag.

Later on, I wished I'd paid more attention.

CHAPTER 2

ON THE BUS

We had to be at school really early on the day we left for Snow Camp. **Mount Impossible**, where the camp was, was at least five hours away. That didn't include stopping for breakfast on the way.

It still looked like night outside when we got on the bus. Joe, Bec, and I managed to get seats in the back of the bus.

Usually Rose Thornton and her friends get the good seats, but Rose was still busy unpacking all her gear from her car when everyone else was ready to go. We watched her from the bus window. **Rose had bags and bags of stuff.**

"How long does she think we're going to be gone?" asked Bec, shaking her head.

"Maybe she's going to stay up there for the **whole winter**," suggested **Joe**.

That thought made me ᕼᗩᑭᑭY.

Finally, the bus took off. It was nice and warm in the bus and really cold outside, so we fogged up the windows pretty quick.

Jake "Monkey Boy" Davern was snoring before we left Bays Park. The last thing I remember was thinking how funny that was. Then the next thing I knew, the sun was shining in through the window and there was DROOL on my T-shirt.

"Oh, good, you're awake," said Joe.

"I wasn't asleep," I said. **My tongue felt like a sheet of cardboard.**

"You were too," said Bec. "You were leaning all over me."

"I'm thirsty," I said, ignoring Bec. "Is anyone else thirsty?"

At eight o'clock we stopped for a breakfast break at Barry & Larry's Motor Diner. I got eggs, bacon, and toast, even though I usually only eat cereal at home. It took the girls about a week to all use the rest rooms. Then, finally, we were back on the bus by nine o'clock.

"This is great," I said, as Joe, Bec, and I headed to our seats in the back of the bus. "If we were in Bays Park now, we'd be at school."

Joe nodded. "Yep, this is GREAT," he said.

"Uh huh," said Bec.

We looked out the window.

"I'm bored," I said.

Joe nodded. "Me too," he said

"Me three," said **Bec**. "How about a game of Twenty Questions?"

"I hate Twenty Questions," said Joe. "You always win."

"No I don't," said Bec with a little smile.

"Come on, Joe. **We can beat her**," I said.

So we spent the next hour playing Twenty Questions.

20 questions

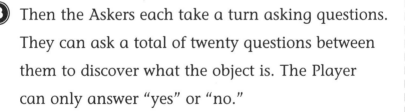
Twenty Questions

1. One person, the Player, writes down the object they are thinking of. This is so they can't change their mind during the game.

2. Once the object is written down on paper, the Askers can ask the Player whether the object is an animal, vegetable, or mineral. (Mineral means something that isn't alive. Vegetable means something that's a plant. Animal means a living creature.)

3. Then the Askers each take a turn asking questions. They can ask a total of twenty questions between them to discover what the object is. The Player can only answer "yes" or "no."

4. If an Asker guesses the object before the twenty questions are up, then that person becomes the Player next and can choose their own object.

I decided that I would be the first Player in our game of Twenty Questions. I was waiting for Bec to ARGUE and say she wanted to be the Player, but she just smiled and said, "Okay."

Joe grabbed a notebook and pen from his backpack. I wrote down my object on a piece of paper, folded it, and placed it on the seat between me and Bec.

"Animal, mineral, or vegetable?" asked Joe.

"Animal," I said.

"**Boris**," said Bec.

I couldn't believe it. Bec had guessed right away that I'd written down my pet dog's name.

"You cheated," I said.

"Did not," said Bec.

"You saw what I wrote down!" I yelled.

"It's my turn," said Bec.

"But you never lose," complained Joe. "I never get to go."

Bec handed Joe the notepad and pen. "Okay," she said. "Your turn."

Joe spent **at least a minute** looking out the window trying to think of something.

"Hurry up, Joe," I said. "We'll be at Snow Camp before we get our next turn."

𝔽𝕀ℕ𝔸𝕃𝕃𝕐 Joe wrote something down. Then he folded the paper into a tiny square.

"Animal, mineral, or vegetable?" asked Joe.

"**We're** supposed to ask that," said Bec. "Not you."

"Oh, right," said Joe.

"So what is it?" I asked.

Joe frowned. "Wait a minute," he said. Then he unfolded the piece of paper, looked at it, and then folded it up again.

"Vegetable," he said finally.

"Carrot?" I asked.

"No," said Joe.

"Potato," said Bec.

Joe turned red. Bec had guessed right again. I couldn't believe it.

"Everyone chooses potato," said Bec.

Then it was her turn.

"Animal, vegetable, or mineral?" asked Joe.

"Vegetable," said Bec.

"Is it a POTATO?" I asked.

"No," said Bec.

"Carrot?" said Joe.

"No," said Bec.

We went through a list of peas, spinach, cauliflower, broccoli, and beans. We kept naming vegetables until we only had two questions left.

"We wasted too many questions asking about specific vegetables," I said. "We need to be more general."

"You're right," said Joe.

"Is it green?" I asked.

"No," said Bec.

"Is it **purple**?" asked Joe suddenly.

"Yes," said Bec. "And that's your twenty questions. I won."

"But I know what it is," said Joe. "It's a **beet**!"

"Too late," said Bec.

"But that's not fair," said Joe.

I could see that they were about to be *in a fight*. I had to think of something to distract them, quick. I tried to think of G𝒜M𝐸S that my parents used to have me and my sister Zoe play in the car when we were little.

They always got sick of us asking, **"how much longer?"** So the games were a way to keep us from thinking about how long it was taking.

All the games I could think of seemed like baby games now, but then I finally thought of one.

"Why don't we play A to Z?" I suggested.

A to Z

A to Z is a great game to play in a car, bus, or train. The aim of the game is to find letters or things that begin with the letters A, B, C, and so on as you work your way through the alphabet. A letter or object cannot be shared.

Each player must find their own letter or object, so players must be quick. The first person to claim an object or a letter can move on to the next letter in the alphabet.

Letters can be found on road signs, bumper stickers, billboards, license plates, etc.

The winner is the first person to reach Z.

Joe turned out to be **really good** at A to Z. He was really quick and kept jumping in before either Bec or I could find anything.

Then he got STUCK on Q for a long time, until Joe noticed a sign that read "Quiet please, hospital zone." That had Q and Z in it. He wasn't allowed to use the Z, though, because he wasn't up to that letter yet.

He got R really quickly. Then, right away, he said, "S!"

"What for?" I asked. I was still only up to M.

Bec pointed to the sign at the side of the road.

"Mount Impossible Snow Camp, 10 miles," she read aloud. "I saw the sign first. Does that mean I win **the whole game**?"

"Bec," said Joe, **"sometimes you go too far."**

NO TV?

I hadn't really noticed that the bus was now climbing up a long hill. The windows of the bus got foggy again as the air outside grew colder.

"S for snow," shouted Bec.

"That wasn't snow," said **Joe**. "That was a plastic bag."

But Bec was right. Dotted along the side of the road, here and there, were globs of snow.

The globs turned into blobs, which turned into larger blobs, which turned into huge sheets of snow covering the ground.

Jake Davern (who we all call "Monkey Boy") let out a monkey cry from the front of the bus and everyone laughed. It was pretty exciting.

Suddenly, I didn't feel tired anymore. I couldn't wait to get out in the snow and throw some snowballs and hit the slopes with my rented snowboard.

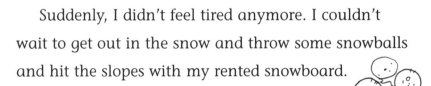

It took another half hour to reach the bus parking lot. By then, a couple of kids were feeling *car sick* after all the winding around the mountain. The bus driver turned the heater off to give us some fresh air. Then it got cold on the bus.

I put on the sweater that Mom had made me put into my backpack. **I'd forgotten how much I hated really cold weather.**

Once we got off the bus, we had to wait forever while the bus was unpacked. Then a couple of SUVs came to take us to our cabin. **I'd already thrown my first snowball,** which was a little muddy from being driven on. **Ms. Stacey** tried to **ban** us from throwing any more snowballs, but that was never going to work.

Rose announced loudly, "It's not really powder snow, is it?"

I got separated from Joe and Bec and ended up in an SUV with Rose and a bunch of her friends. The girls kept **screeching** and **GIGGLING** every time the car went over a large bump or jolted to the left or right. I couldn't hear anything over their **screaming**.

Paul Jurkovic was sitting next to me. He was riding out the uneven trip **like he was on a surfboard.**

"Cool," he kept saying.

Jake Davern was hanging onto the overhead strap like a **monkey**.

Meanwhile, I was hanging onto my seat just so I wouldn't crash into Rose.

"Isn't this cool?" Paul asked me.

I could only nod, because my teeth were CHATTERING so much from the cold.

Once we got to the cabin, we raced inside to pick out our rooms. I was walking down the hallway of the boys' wing when **Joe** stuck his head out through a doorway.

"Here, David," he said.

There were two sets of bunk beds in the room. Joe had grabbed one of the two top bunks and set up his sleeping bag and pillow to claim it as his own. I grabbed the other top bunk. There was a window between our beds that looked out over the ski runs.

I watched a couple of snowboarders carve a perfect path through the snow.

"That's going to be **you and me**, Joe," I said. "We'll be Mogul Munchers before you know it."

"For sure," said Joe, nodding wisely. "So, what is a Mogul Muncher, David?"

* * *

After we ate lunch, we bought our lift tickets.  **You have to have them to get up the hills.** Then the people with their own skis and boards went in one direction. The rest of us got fitted for our gear.

"Who's in your room?" I asked Bec as we waited in line.

Bec was wearing a pink ski suit with **fluffy stuff** around the hood. My jacket didn't have any fluff, luckily, but it did have lots of zips and pockets. And my ski pants were waterproof. That made me wonder if I should test how waterproof they were by spilling a drink over them.

"Bonnie, Steph, and Kaya," answered Bec. "Are you staying with Joe?"

I nodded. "And Paul and Jake," I answered.

Then it was Bec's turn at the front of the line. Bec decided she wanted to rent skis.

"No way," I said. "Come on, Bec. Snowboards are **much more fun**."

"Skis look **easier**," said Bec. "I'm sticking with them."

The guy who helped me wanted to give me skis too.

"I'm a Mogul Muncher," I said casually. "So, you'd better give me a snowboard. I don't want to be BORED out there."

The guy whistled. "Mogul Muncher, huh?" he said. "Have you ever skied before?"

I shook my head.

"Okay," he said. "Here you go."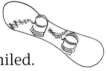
He handed me my snowboard and smiled.

By the time I got out on the slopes, I'd missed the afternoon lesson. It probably didn't matter, because **I could hardly stand up on my board.**

My boots were locked into position. Every time I tried to walk, **I fell over.** And icy snow is not as soft as it looks.

Bec and Joe both made it to their lessons, so I just hung around at the bottom of the slope. I took one foot out of a boot and tried to use the snowboard like a skateboard. That was fun, except it made my foot 𝕅𝕌𝕄𝔹 from the icy cold snow.

Rose Thornton passed me a few times on the way to the ski lift, but I pretended not to see her showing off. Even though she was speaking really loudly so everyone could hear her. **I tried to block her out**, but I kept hearing parts of what she was saying.

". . . in the Alps, when I was there last . . ."

and

". . . won that race, but time trials really aren't my thing . . ."

and

". . . about a thousand dollars, but it's really good quality so it's worth it . . ."

I was glad to get back to our cabin and change into some warm socks. My foot finally thawed by the end of dinner. Then we realized that **the cabin didn't have a TV.**

"What? No TV?" wailed Joe.

He was freaking out. I had to slap him on the back to get him out of it.

I realized that I should have brought the board games that Mom had suggested after all. "There are plenty of things we can do without a TV," I said.

"What?" said Joe. "What could we possibly do?"

I looked at Rose Thornton.

"Detective in the Dark," I said with a smile.

CHAPTER 4

DETECTIVE IN THE DARK

Detective in the Dark was one of my **all-time favorite games**. I asked a couple of kids if they wanted to play with us.

Then **Rose** found out, and she said she didn't want to play. I said that was fine because I hadn't asked her. Then she went to tell Ms. Stacey.

I'm sure she thought Ms. Stacey would tell us *we couldn't play*, but Ms. Stacey just clapped her hands and said that Detective in the Dark had been her favorite game when she was a kid.

Mr. Mildendew, our gym teacher, said he was the king of Detective in the Dark and would teach everyone how to play it.

A couple of the girls said they were **too scared** to play, so Joe said he would stay with them in the dining room and play cards. I thought that was pretty nice of him. **I know how much he would have wanted to join in on the fun.**

Detective in the Dark

You will need: paper, pen

① On a sheet of notepaper, write an X. Fold the paper over several times so the writing is hidden. On another piece of paper, write the word "detective." On new sheets of paper, write your own words (like "brother," "sister," "aunt," "father," "salesman," "butler," etc.). Put all of the pieces of paper in a hat and have everyone choose one.

② The person who receives the paper scrap with the word "detective" needs to leave the room. As they leave, they should turn off the lights. (*Make sure you play this game in an open space where there aren't too many obstacles. Also make sure that the room is as dark as possible.*)

③ Everyone hides.

④ Then the person who got the X finds a victim.

⑤ Once a victim is tapped on the shoulder, they must scream and lie on the floor. The detective returns to the room and turns on the light.

6 The detective then talks to no more than eight suspects. The detective should ask the suspects questions like:

- Where were you standing when the victim screamed?

- Are you related to the victim?

- Have you ever met the victim before?

- Did you like the victim?

- Have you had any recent fights with the victim?

- What do you stand to gain from the victim's death?

7 Each person can reveal their character if they wish (except for X, of course, who will not want to) and they can make up their own story about their relationship with the victim. This could lead to many suspects. Everyone can have an idea about who X is, but the detective is the one who must decide.

8 If the detective guesses correctly, the detective wins the game. If the detective guesses wrong, X wins.

Ms. Stacey decided that the game room was the best place to hold the game. She made sure all the curtains were closed so that no light could come into the room. I was really hoping to get the paper that said "detective." Instead I got the paper that said "**butler.**"

Jake Davern got the detective paper, so he had to leave the room. Mr. Mildendew stood near the light switch, just in case things got out of hand and we had to turn on the light quickly.

"Are we ready?" he asked.

Everyone nodded and a couple of kids giggled, including Luke Firth, who seemed just **a little bit nervous.**

Mr. Mildendew turned off the light. I could hear people moving around, trying to find a safe place where X wouldn't find them in the dark.

Someone brushed past me and I shrank back into the curtains to stay out of their way. Then there was a piercing scream. **I was sure it was Rose Thornton, being dramatic.**

Mr. Mildendew snapped on the light. I was surprised to see Ms. Stacey lying on the floor. I would have been WORRIED, but she had a huge grin on her face.

Then Jake marched through the door and said, "I believe there's been a *crime* here!"

"Well done, detective," said Rose.

Jake pointed to Rose. "And it was you," he said.

"It was not," said Rose. "Anyway, **you have to ask questions first.**"

I already had a story made up that would make me look really guilty. But Jake didn't get around to asking me.

He did ask Chris Lang, who said that he was a brother of the victim and had just had an argument with her the night before about using **the last squirt of the toothpaste.**

Then Jake asked Lee Hall, who said he had never seen the victim before, though she did look COOL. (This made some of the girls giggle and Ms. Stacey smile even wider, but she still kept her eyes closed.)

Then Jake asked **Kaya Cheung** what her favorite color was.

Kaya seemed confused and said, "Red."

"That's right," said Jake. "Red — the color of your face. **I do believe I found the X!**"

Everyone laughed. Kaya just nodded and said, "Yep. It was me."

Ms. Stacey got off the floor. I patted Jake on the back. "Not bad," I said.

Jake did a little monkey dance and said, "Yeah. Well."

Then we played again until it was time for hot chocolate and bed.

Back in the dining room, the girls had beaten Joe at cards. He didn't seem to mind too much.

"You really missed a good game," I told him.

Joe shrugged. **"Maybe next time,"** he said.

I climbed into my top bunk. After our light had been turned off, I opened the curtains to look out the window.

"Hey, Joe," I said. "Look, **it's snowing**."

"Cool," said Joe.

I watched the huge flakes falling down like feathers until I fell asleep.

CHAPTER 5

When I woke up the next morning, it was still pretty dark. I slipped out of bed, got dressed quickly, and made my way to the kitchen.

Mrs. Ellis, Stephanie's mom and our parent helper, was making us a **huge batch of pancakes** for breakfast.

"Good morning, David," she said. "Hot chocolate?"

Could life get any better?

I was sitting at the breakfast bar when Mr. Mildendew burst through the front door, snow whirling in with him. He stamped his boots on the rug. Then he took them off and put them in the drying room.

"Now **that** is a snowstorm," Mr. Mildendew said.

"Snowstorm?" I asked.

"Take a look outside," Mr. Mildendew said.

I went to the dining room windows and pulled back the curtains. Outside was just **a swirl of white**. There was no hint of the ski runs that lay beyond our cabin.

"COOL," I said. "A real snowstorm."

By the time breakfast was ready, everyone was up and dressed.

"I've never been in a big snowstorm before," said **Joe**. "This reminds me of a movie."

Joe's parents owned a DVD store, and he got to watch a lot of movies.

"I'm not sure what it was called," said Joe, "but these people were stuck in a snowstorm, and they met the Abdominal Snowman—"

"I think you mean Abominable Snowman," said Bec. "Abdominal means something about your stomach."

"Yeah, that," said Joe. "Anyway, the snowman was **eating** them one by one—"

"Quiet for a moment, please," said Ms. Stacey.

Everyone stopped talking. It was so quiet I could hear the soft swish of snow hitting the windows.

"Well, as you can see, we're in the middle of a blizzard," said **Ms. Stacey**. "Unless things clear up this afternoon, we will not be going outside today."

Everyone groaned.

"But there's no TV," Carly Johnson called out. "What are we going to do all day?"

"I do have some schoolwork with me," began Ms. Stacey.

More groans.

"Or you can keep yourselves AMUSED, as long as you behave yourselves," Ms. Stacey said.

Everyone agreed that this was the best idea. Some kids stayed in the dining room and had a second breakfast. Other kids

wandered back to their rooms to read or just hang out with their friends. I went to the game room with Joe and Bec.

"This is the worst," said Joe.

"Definitely," said Bec.

"Are you kidding?" I said. "We're on VACATION. During school time."

"But no skiing," said Bec.

"Or snowboarding," said Joe.

"Okay, that's **not cool**," I said. "But there's also **no schoolwork**."

"Or TV," said Joe.

Bec threw a pillow at Joe. Then I threw a cushion at her. We would have thrown more, but Mr. Mildendew walked past the game room so we sat up straight and **pretended** we were just talking.

"Let's play cards," said Joe after Mr. Mildendew passed by.

We played a game of Go Fish until Joe got bored. A few other people joined in as we played.

"Let's play Pass It On," suggested **Kaya**.

"Great!" said Joe.

If he'd known what Pass It On was, **he might not have been so excited to play.**

Pass It On

The aim of Pass It On is to pass an orange down a line of people without dropping it. The hard part is that it's **no hands allowed**.

1. Form two equal teams.

2. The teams must line up boy, girl, boy, girl unless there is more of one group than of another.

3. The orange is tucked under the chin of the first person of each team and passed on to the next person in the line behind them.

4. When the orange gets to the last person, they must run to the front of the line with the orange still tucked under their chin. They must then pass the orange back to the person in line behind them.

5. This continues until everyone is back in his or her original position in the line.

6. If the orange falls to the ground, the orange must go to the front of the line and start again.

Hints:

1 Make sure everyone eats a mint before the game begins. There is nothing like bad breath to make someone drop an orange.

2 If the team members next to each other in line are too different in height, the taller person could crouch down before trying to pass the orange.

3 If the orange starts to fall, think about other parts of your body that you can use to help get the orange back up to your chin. The person who you are passing to can also help tuck the orange back under your chin, as long as they don't use their hands. Elbows can be really helpful.

Kaya got some more students to play. Then she divided us into two teams, lining us up boy, then girl, then boy until everyone was in line.

There were more boys than girls, so there were a couple of boys together at the end of both lines.

Joe and I were at the end of the first line. That was fine with me. **I didn't want to pass an orange to a girl.**

Ms. Stacey grabbed her digital camera to take photos. Mrs. Ellis kept cracking up because she thought we looked so 𝔽𝕌ℕℕ𝕐.

At the head of our line was Rose Thornton. Luke Firth was next in line after her. Rose was busy bossing Luke around and trying to tell him the best way to pass the orange when Kaya yelled "Start!"

Bec was the leader of the second line. She quickly passed her orange to Paul with no problems. Paul passed it, not so quickly, to Stephanie. She almost dropped it, but managed to keep it at the last minute.

Luke was so busy laughing that he dropped the orange, and Rose had to start again.

That made Rose mad.

The orange had already gone to the front of the other line when Joe finally turned to me with the orange tucked under his chin.

"Ready?" he asked.

I nodded and leaned in to grab the orange from under Joe's chin. Then I ran to the start of the line.

That's when I realized that I had to pass it to Rose.

I took a deep breath. As I leaned forward to pass the orange to Rose, someone said, "He's gonna kiss her."

Then I dropped the orange.

CHAPTER 6

QUALITY TIME

Everyone was still talking about the Pass It On game when we sat down for lunch.

Mrs. Ellis and a couple of helpers had made lots of huge sandwiches and vats of hot chocolate. I made sure I sat far away from Rose so I didn't have to **look her in the eye.**

"That was a really close game," said Joe, munching on a sandwich.

I just grunted and watched the snow swirling outside the dining room window.

"I think we really lost when **you dropped the orange**," began Joe.

"I wonder if we'll be able to go outside today," I interrupted.

"I doubt it," said Bec. "**Too bad**, because I was really getting the hang of those skis."

"You **HATED** skiing," said Joe.

"How would you know?" said Bec. "You were too busy **falling over all the time** to worry about anyone else."

"Well, I was pretty much a NATURAL on the snowboard," I said. "It's too bad you didn't see me. Oh well. **Here's to spending quality time with my friends.**" Then I raised my mug of hot chocolate.

"Quality time," echoed Joe and Bec.

And we clinked mugs.

I was on kitchen duty that day for lunch and dinner. It took me about an hour to finish drying the dishes and cleaning up before I left the kitchen. When I was done, I found Joe and Bec back in the game room.

"Oh, good," said Bec. "Here's David."

"I am NOT passing an orange to **Rose's chin**," I said, holding up my hands.

"No oranges," Bec said. "Let's play Mixed Signals."

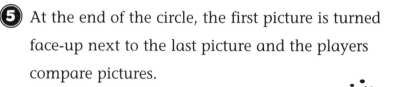

Mixed Signals

Each player must have a piece of paper and a pen or pencil.

 The group should form a circle, sitting on the floor.

 The first person draws a simple picture and shows it to the person next to them. That person has 20 seconds to look at the picture, then the first picture is turned face down.

 The second player must then draw the same picture and show it to the person next to them.

 The third player again has 20 seconds to look at the picture before redrawing it on their paper, and so on.

5 At the end of the circle, the first picture is turned face-up next to the last picture and the players compare pictures.

There were about 12 kids in the game room who wanted to play. We all sat in a circle.

Bec started the game because **she's so good** at drawing. I was the last person in the circle, so I tried to draw exactly what Joe (who was next to me) had drawn and shown me.

"Okay, here's my picture," said Bec. She held up a really cool cartoon RAT. "Show us your picture, David."

I held up a picture of a sailboat.

"Um, I think something went **wrong**," I said.

CHAPTER 7

THE ABDOMINABLE SNOWMAN

All day long, the snow swirled outside our cabin windows. It looked so **cold and frosty** out there, but it was **warm and toasty** inside so I didn't mind too much.

"How long do you think a person could 𝕊𝕌ℝ𝕍𝕀𝕍𝔼 out there?" I asked Joe.

"Depends," said Joe. "If you were wearing shorts, probably not too long. But if you were wearing a snowsuit, you could probably survive for a lot longer. Like at least a few hours."

"What do you think would happen?" said Bec.

"Well, I think your fingers and toes would **freeze** first," I said.

I had watched a documentary about mountain climbers once. Their fingers had turned black from frostbite. *It was pretty gross.* When my mom caught me watching it, she made me turn it off.

"Do you think **your blood** would freeze?" asked **Bec**.

"My blood would freeze if I saw the Abdominable Snowman!" Joe said.

"Joe, it's not Abdominable!" Bec said.

"I know," Joe told her. "But how 𝒞𝒪𝒪ℒ would it be to take a picture of one? Imagine how much money that would be worth. Or get one on film — that would be even better. **Then you could prove that it was really real.**"

"The Abominable Snowman is not real," said Bec.

"Well, anyway, what if we get snowed in here for a week? **That would be so cool!**" said **Joe**. "We could miss out on a whole week of school!"

"That doesn't make sense," Bec pointed out. "A week goes for seven days, and we only go to school five days a week."

"Oh, yeah," said Joe.

"And if we stayed longer than four days, we could **run out of food**," I said.

"Really?" said Joe. "I didn't think of that."

We had a snack around three o'clock. Then, just when we were wondering what to do next, **Mr. Mildendew** said, "Let's play Balloon Bust."

"Hey, yeah!" said Jake, who was jumping around like a monkey with **ants in his pants**. Not that monkeys wear pants.

Mr. Mildendew just happened to have some balloons and string with him. "I always carry balloons with me," he said. "Just for **emergencies**," he explained.

About ten of us decided we wanted to play. We moved the furniture to the edges of the game room so we had a wide open space. Then we each got a balloon and had to blow it up.

I'd played the game before, so I made sure not to blow up my balloon too much.

Joe kept blowing so much that he POPPED his balloon and had to get another one.

Balloon Bust

You will need:

- One balloon per person and a couple more for emergencies.

- String for each person, about 18 inches long

The idea of this game is to burst the balloon of your opponents without getting your own balloon burst. The last person left with a balloon is the winner.

How to play:

Blow up your balloon. Then tie it (loosely, so it won't hurt your ankle) to your leg. Then run around like crazy, trying to burst other players' balloons.

Note:

Balloon Bust is best played in areas with a lot of open space.

Once we each had a blown-up balloon, we tied our balloons to our ankles.

Mr. Mildendew had decided to play, so everyone was trying to stay out of his way. That's because he had **really long legs** and it was easy for him to BURST someone else's balloon.

Everyone was running around the room, trying to jump on balloons and trying to keep their own balloons safe.

Luke Firth decided he would stay in the corner and keep his balloon safe, until Mr. Mildendew saw what he was doing and **burst** it himself.

Jake Davern got so excited he **burst** his own balloon, thinking he was jumping on someone else's.

We actually got so hot running around that the windows got all steamed up in the game room. I started to sweat.

It was really loud too. Not only were balloons popping like a big batch of POPCORN, but we were all laughing and screaming. I wonder what it sounded like to people outside the game room.

At some point in the game, someone had to turn the lights on because the afternoon light was so dim and it was hard for us to see anything.

Of course Mr. Mildendew won.

We all wanted a chance for a **revenge** game, but some of us were on kitchen duty and had to help get dinner ready.

After dinner, we thought about what to play next. Someone suggested Truth or Dare.

"No way!" I said. I wasn't worried about the *dares*, but I didn't like the idea of telling my **truths** to my whole class.

Then Luke Firth suggested that we play a game of Sardines. Mrs. Ellis suggested we wait for our dinner to go down, so we waited five minutes.

It was the longest five minutes of my life.

Sardines

This is Hide and Seek with a twist.

1 Choose one person to be IT. The rest of the group closes their eyes and counts to 60 while IT finds somewhere to hide. This game does not have to be kept to just one room.

2 Once the group has counted to 60, each player goes off in search of IT. Once a player finds IT, they need to wait until the coast is clear, then go into IT's hiding place and hide there too. One by one, players will begin to disappear from the search group until there is only one searcher left. This is the end of the game.

3 The first person who found IT is now the new IT and a new game begins.

Hint:

If you're IT, make sure you choose a spot where plenty of players can squash in beside you.

Rose Thornton joined in this game, so **of course she had to be bossy** about the rules, even though it was Luke's idea.

"No going into bunk rooms," said Rose. "And no going into bathrooms."

Someone laughed.

"I'm serious," said **Rose**. "Or I will have to tell Ms. Stacey."

There was a rumble through the group. Then someone piped up and said, "Okay."

Everyone voted that I should be IT. **I guess that's what I got for being so popular**. While everyone faced the game room wall and counted to 60, I scooted off to find a place to hide.

I ended up hiding in the pantry. I'd spent so much time on kitchen duty, I'd had time to check it out. The pantry was pretty roomy, except for the sack of potatoes on the floor and the large cans of flour and sugar.

I closed the door in time. Then I heard the sound of footsteps thumping across the cabin floors.

The first person to find me was Jake Davern, and that was only because he'd snuck into the kitchen to get a snack. He stood in the open pantry doorway **staring** at me. I pulled him inside and shut the door.

"No one's supposed to find us," I said.

"Oh. Okay," said Jake.

We snacked on some potato chips until the next person came along.

It took about half an hour before the **last person** opened the door. Of course, that person was Rose Thornton. "What are you doing in here?" she screeched.

It was hard to answer her, because I had Paul's elbow digging into my ribs and Kaya's ponytail tickling my nose.

"The pantry was *off limits*," shouted **Rose**.

Everyone said that only the bedrooms and bathrooms had been off limits, but Rose wouldn't listen. **She refused to be IT**. So that was the end of Sardines.

CHAPTER 8

NIGHT OF THE MISSING ROOMMATE

Since Rose wouldn't play Sardines, **we weren't sure what to do.** So we sat in the pantry for a little while. We ate some more potato chips, but soon we were bored.

"What should we do now?" someone asked.

For a while, no one said anything.

"Does anyone know *Night of the Living Mummy?*" someone piped up from near the bag of potatoes. "We could play that."

"I do," yelled Jake. "And we need lots of toilet paper. To the bathrooms!"

Rose Thornton made us ask **Ms. Stacey** if we could use the toilet paper before we could start the game. Ms. Stacey made sure that there would be enough paper left. Then she let us have ten rolls.

The Night of the Living Mummy

The group needs to be split into two teams. Each team is given 5 rolls of toilet paper.

Choose a team member to wrap in toilet paper so that they end up looking like an mummy. The event lasts for two minutes. Once the two minutes is up, the winner is the team that has the neatest and most-wrapped mummy.

Hints:

(1) If your chosen mummy team member wears glasses, they should remove their glasses before being wrapped up.

(2) Think about Egyptian mummies. Their arms are usually by their side and their legs are wrapped together. This is probably an easier way than trying to wrap the limbs separately.

(3) Make sure you leave some gaps for the mummy to breathe through.

(4) Make sure you ask an adult if it's okay to use the toilet paper before you play this game. Otherwise they might get mad!

We split into two groups, but my group wasn't doing very well. We'd chosen to wrap Jake up as the mummy, but he kept trying to do his monkey dance. That kept breaking the toilet paper.

Then Ms. Stacey came into the room. She said **game time was over.** We had to get ready for bed.

I brushed my teeth and climbed onto my top bunk, leaving my socks on as I slipped into my sleeping bag.

Joe's bunk was empty. **How long did it take to brush your teeth?**

My roommates were already snoring when I slipped out of bed and padded to the boys' bathroom. The light was still on, but Joe wasn't there. I felt his toothbrush. It was dry.

STRANGE.

I looked in the game room, but it was empty. In the dining area, Ms. Stacey, Mr. Mildendew, and Mrs. Ellis were sitting around a table, drinking coffee.

"What's up, David?" asked Mr. Mildendew.

"It's Joe," I said. "He's missing."

Mr. Mildendew checked out Joe's bunk. Then he looked in all the bathrooms. But when Mr. Mildendew came back, Joe wasn't with him.

Ms. Stacey took a flashlight and looked into all the rooms. A couple of kids came into the dining room to find out what was going on.

"Why am I awake?" demanded Rose, stomping out of her room.

"Joe's missing," said Paul.

"He's probably just looking for a TV," said Rose.

No one laughed.

Bec walked over to me. She whispered, "What if Joe went outside to look for the **Abominable Snowman**?" she asked.

"No way," I said. "It's way too cold out there. It's night time. And Ms. Stacey said we weren't allowed outside without a buddy. **I'm Joe's buddy.** He wouldn't go without me."

"When was the last time we saw him?" asked Bec.

"The Mummy Game," I said.

"No. Joe wasn't at the Mummy Game," said Bec.

"Are you sure?" I asked.

"Positive," said Bec.

"Sardines?" I suggested.

Bec shook her head. "He wasn't in the pantry at the end of the game," she said.

"Are you sure?" I asked.

"Yeah, David," Bec said nervously.

"He wouldn't go looking for the Abominable Snowman," I said. **But I wasn't sure I believed that anymore.**

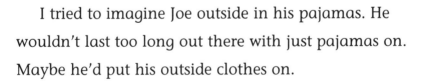

I tried to imagine Joe outside in his pajamas. He wouldn't last too long out there with just pajamas on. Maybe he'd put his outside clothes on.

"We have to tell Ms. Stacey," said Bec.

"Just let me check the drying room," I said.

If Joe's snowsuit was gone, then I would know for sure that he was outside looking for the Abominable Snowman.

Bec followed me into the drying room. It was warm in there. Joe's snowsuit was still hanging up where he'd left it.

"His suit's still here," I told Bec.

Just then there was a rustle behind some coats and **Joe's head popped out.** It looked like he'd just woken up.

"**Does that mean I'm IT?**" he asked.

* * *

It turned out that Joe had gotten CONFUSED about the Sardines game. He'd thought he had to go and hide, so he chose the drying room and settled down behind the coats. The room had been so warm that Joe had fallen asleep waiting to be found.

"Can I go back to bed now?" demanded **Rose** after Joe told us all what had happened.

Joe **apologized** to everyone. Then we all went back to bed. When Joe and I settled down in our sleeping bags, I opened the curtains to check the weather. The snow was still whirling around outside.

"Well, that was EXCITING," I said finally.

"Not really," said Joe. "I just fell asleep."

"Yeah," I said. "Bec and I thought you'd gone looking for the Abdominal Snowman," I whispered.

"It's Abominable," corrected Joe. "As if I'd do anything that stupid. **It's cold out there!**"

I watched the snow whirling for a while longer.

"Yeah, well, I'm glad you didn't," I said.

But the only reply was Joe snoring.

CHAPTER 9

SNOWED IN

The next day, day three, **Mr. Mildendew** put his snowsuit on and left the cabin to find out more information about the storm. When he got back, **he didn't look happy.**

"The weather station said that the storm isn't changing," said Mr. Mildendew. "If it doesn't change soon, we may be stuck up here for another day."

"But **what if we run out of food?**" yelled Jake, who was eating his third helping of pancakes.

"Then we can blame you," said Mr. Mildendew.

"But what are we going to do all day?" whined **Rose**. She was wearing one of her many ski outfits, just in case we could go outside.

"Well," said Mr. Mildendew. "Ms. Stacey, Mrs. Ellis, and I have planned a day full of activities that will **knock your socks off!**"

We all cheered.

Treasure Hunt

You will need:

- Paper and pens.

- Someone to write clues (one set for each team) and judge whether the treasures that are found are acceptable. There should be ten clues for each team.

- A couple of teams (as many as you want).

- The aim of the game is to find — or make — treasures from all the clues you are given before the other teams are done. The first team to have all the treasures wins.

A list of suggested treasures to collect (or make):

Something red.

Something that melts.

An ingredient you would find on a pizza.

Something with wheels. ➡

Something you find in the sea. *(Salt, sand, shell, fish — you could use a fish stick, cut out a fish from a magazine, or draw a fish, for example.)*

Something that keeps the rain off. *(A hat, umbrella, coat, or be more inventive like a saucepan lid, a plastic bag etc.)*

Something for good luck.

You can also scramble the clues for Treasure Hunt. Here are some examples:

tuorshtboh (toothbrush)

ruaribhsh (hairbrush)

urlre (ruler)

tobos (boots)

aht (hat)

Memory Cards

Memory Cards is pretty simple. All you need is a deck of cards.

1. Lay all of the cards face down on a flat surface. The first player turns over two cards.

2. If the player turns up a pair — for example, two cards with the number 8 printed on them — then the player takes the pair and gets another turn.

3. This is a great game for two or more players. You could also use more than one pack of cards to extend the game to more players.

The game ends when there are no more face-down cards left.

The player with the most pairs wins the game.

Mind Ball

This is a game for three or more players. You will need a light ball to play this game.

1 Players sit in a circle on the floor.

2 The first person in the circle (you choose) decides on a category such as food, cities, movies, colors, etc.

3 Then that person throws the ball to another person in the circle (it can be anyone).

4 The person who catches the ball must name an item in the chosen category and throw the ball to someone else.

5 If a player catching the ball cannot think of an item within ten seconds, or repeats something that has already been said, they are out of the game and need to leave the circle.

6 The person to the left of the player who named the first category must choose the next category.

7 The goal of the game is to be the last person left in the circle.

Hints:

If you don't have a light ball to throw around the circle, you can use any small light object, such as a rolled-up pair of socks or bag of split peas (make sure these bags are put in several plastic bags and tied in case they break).

You could write up a whole list of subjects on a piece of paper, then tear each subject off, fold it in half, and put it in the middle of the circle. When it is time for a new category, it is selected from the pieces of folded paper in the middle.

CHAPTER 10

MOGUL MUNCHERS

By the time we were done playing Mind Ball, it was time for lunch.

Mrs. Ellis had made some pizzas. She told us all to go and wash our hands before we ate. By the time we got back to the dining area, there was **no food** to be seen.

"I knew it," said Jake. **"We've run out of food. We're all going to starve."**

"No way," Rose said. But she looked pretty nervous about it.

I was confused. "I can smell the pizza, but seeing it is a different story," I said.

"They won't let us starve," **Bec** said. "But I am getting pretty hungry."

Mrs. Ellis appeared in the doorway.

"Well, are you hungry or not?" she asked.

Then she led us into the game room, where she'd set up a picnic on the floor. Somehow it was **even more fun** than a real picnic outside.

"No ants," explained Joe.

I think that helped.

After lunch we played a game called **Mogul Munchers**. I finally had to ask someone what a mogul was, so I asked Mr. Mildendew. He explained it to me.

Mogul: A mogul is a bump on a ski slope. It is created when lots of skiers turn at the same spot on the path and snow is pushed up into a mound.

Well, no wonder my dad looked so proud when he told me about his nickname. **Riding moguls** sounded hard. I didn't even want to think about snowboarding down them.

Thankfully, our game Mogul Munchers wasn't nearly as hard.

Mogul Munchers

The object of this game is to dress up in ski gear, run through a ski course, and take off the ski gear at the end of the course. The first team to have every team member complete the course is the winner.

You will need:

- Two teams.

- Ski overalls, scarf, gloves, jacket, hat, and goggles.

- You will also need to create four large "snow moguls" out of cardboard (i.e. circles of cardboard large enough for a person to stand on). Each team gets two.

How to play:

Break your teams into two parts. One half of each team is located at one end of the room and the other half is located at the opposite end of the room. There is only one set of ski gear per team.

The game begins at one end of the room when one person yells "**Go**."

One team member from each team at that end of the room needs to get dressed in the ski gear.

Once dressed, those two players pick up the "moguls." The players throw one mogul out in front of them on the ground. They must then jump on the mogul.

Then they throw the next mogul in front of them and jump to that.

Then they reach back and grab the first mogul. They throw that out in front of them and jump onto that.

They repeat these actions until they reach their team members on the opposite side of the room.

Then the first players remove the ski gear.

One of their team members must put on the ski gear and complete the mogul course back to their team on the opposite side of the room.

This continues until the last player from the team has completed the course and removed their ski gear.

You don't have to use skiing as the theme for Mogul Munchers. You can choose your own "theme" for this game. It could be a football theme, or a jungle theme, an island theme, or . . . make up your own theme! Once you've chosen your theme, choose equipment that fit it. For example, for a jungle theme . . .

You will need:

- A hat, sunglasses, binoculars (make your own out of paper towel roll), jacket, and backpack.

- You will also need to create "stepping stones" out of cardboard.

The idea for this game is that you use the "stones" to cross the piranha-filled river while wearing jungle gear.

The game is played the same way.

Mogul Munchers was **really fun.** Our team had Mr. Mildendew's ski overalls and half the kids kept *tripping* because his overalls were so big.

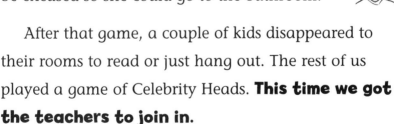

Rose Thornton almost didn't play because she wanted to wear her own ski gear. She complained that the other ski clothes didn't fit right. Mr. Mildendew had to explain that wearing clothes that were too 𝔅𝕀𝔾 was part of the fun.

Then Rose started complaining that clothes smelled funny. These clothes belonged to our teachers! Didn't she realize that it was **rude** to say their clothes smelled?

Bec laughed over Rose so much she had to be excused so she could go to the bathroom.

After that game, a couple of kids disappeared to their rooms to read or just hang out. The rest of us played a game of Celebrity Heads. **This time we got the teachers to join in.**

Celebrity Heads

Choose five players to be "celebrities." All of the celebrities should sit in chairs lined up in the middle of the room.

The audience (the rest of the players) writes down the names of five famous people. Each name is attached to a hat or headband.

The celebrities are each given a hat or headband with a name on it. They can see the names on the other celebrities' hats, but not their own name.

The first person to guess their celebrity name is the winner. The celebrities have to ask the audience questions to find out who they are.

Hint:

It's easier to ask right up front whether you are a male or female celebrity.

For the first round, Mr. Mildendew's celebrity name was *Joan of Arc*, Ms. Stacey was **Albert Einstein**, Paul was **Big Bird**, Joe was **Neil Armstrong**, and Rose was **George Washington**.

Ms. Stacey won, and Paul said there was no way he ever would have figured out that he was **Big Bird**.

We had so much fun we played another round. Then another.

Halfway through the third round, **Mrs. Ellis** came to the game room. Next to her was one of the people who were in charge of Snow Camp.

"Hi folks," he said. "Just thought I'd pass on the news. The weather's clearing so we'll be running the lifts tomorrow morning. Looks like you'll get in some **action on the slopes** after all."

Everyone cheered. **Then we went back to our game.**

That night after dinner, we played 20/20 Vision.

20/20 Vision

This game is played in the dark.

You'll need:

- A flashlight.

One person should be IT. IT will hold the flashlight.

Home base is in the middle of the room.

The aim of the game is to make it to home base without IT seeing you.

IT cannot move from home base. He or she must shine the flashlight from there.

The first person back to home base without being seen is the winner.

Step One:

All players start at home base, including IT.

Step Two:

The light is turned off. IT must count to 60 (1 cat and dog, 1 cat and dog) to allow the players to hide.

Step Three:

IT turns on the flashlight and shines the light around the room.

If IT spots someone, IT yells, "20/20, I see David!" (or whoever they see). Then that person must come back to home base, and they are out of the game. They should sit on the floor to show that they are out of the game.

Step Four:

Continue until everyone is back at home base. The last person caught by IT, or the last person who makes it back without being spotted, is the next IT.

Hint:

It's a good idea to play this game in a room without too many obstacles or things that might be broken. Things like vases or dogs should be removed before the game begins.

It's also a good idea to wear dark colors that blend into the shadows. That way you're less likely to be spotted by the flashlight.

We played until **Jake Davern fell asleep**  while he was IT. Then we all went to bed.

* * *

The next day, we were able to ski and snowboard until early afternoon. The good thing about the snowstorm was that it had dumped tons of powder snow in all the right places. It didn't hurt so much when I fell over, which I did **most of the time.**

By the time we got on the bus that afternoon, **I could have slept for a week.**

My body was hurting all over from falling down so much and using muscles I didn't know I had.

I was even too tired to play "I Spy" with Joe and Bec.

"That was **the best trip ever**," Bec said as the bus wound its way down Mount Impossible.

"Yeah," I said. "It was."

Joe nodded. "The only thing that would have made it better would be if we'd seen an **Abominable Snowman**," he said.

"It just goes to show you," said Bec. "We don't need TV at all. In fact, **we should never turn on a TV again!**"

"Bec," said Joe, "**sometimes you go too far.**"

And I agreed.

About the Author

When Karen Tayleur was growing up, her father told her many stories about his own childhood. These stories continued to grow. She says, "I always enjoyed the retelling, and wanted to create a character who had the same abilities with 'bending the truth.'" And David Mortimore Baxter was born! Karen lives in Australia with her husband, two children, two cats, and one dog.

About the Illustrator

Brann Garvey lives in Minneapolis, Minnesota, with his wife, Keegan, their dog, Lola, and their very fat cat, Iggy. Brann graduated from Iowa State University with a bachelor of fine arts degree. He later attended the Minneapolis College of Art and Design, where he studied illustration. In his free time, Brann enjoys being with his family and friends. He brings his sketchbook everywhere he goes.

Glossary

Abominable Snowman (uh-BOM-uh-nuh-buhl SNOH-man)—a mythical, hair-covered man said to live in snowy areas

ban (BAN)—to forbid something

category (KAT-uh-gor-ee)—a group of things that has something in common

dramatic (druh-MAT-ik)—if someone is being dramatic, they are making too much fuss about something

natural (NACH-ur-uhl)—if you're a natural at something, you're good at it without having to be taught how to do it

numb (NUHM)—unable to feel anything

object (OB-jikt)—something you can see and touch but that is not alive

obstacle (OB-stuh-kuhl)—something in the way

quality time (KWAHL-uh-tee TIME)—special time spent with friends or family

survive (sur-VIVE)—to stay alive through a dangerous event

suspect (SUHSS-pekt)—someone thought to be responsible for a crime

victim (VIK-tuhm)—the person to whom a crime happens

Discussion Questions

1. As a group, talk about the games that David and his friends play in this book. What other games could they have played?

2. When he notices that Joe is missing, did David do the right thing? What else could he have done?

3. Would you enjoy a four-day trip with your schoolmates? Why or why not? Talk about your answers!

Writing Prompts

1. Choose one of the games in this book. Play it with your friends. Then write about what happened. Don't forget to include whether there was a winner of the game!

2. If you were snowed in on a school trip, what would you do to keep yourself busy? Write about it.

3. David wants to learn to snowboard, even though he's never tried. Write about something you'd like to learn.

David Mortimore Baxter

David is a great kid, but he has one big problem — he can't stop talking. These wildly humorous stories, told by David himself, will show readers just how much trouble a boy and his mouth can get into, whether he's going on a class trip, trying to find a missing neighbor, running a detective agency, or getting lost in the wild. David is amiable, engaging, cool, and smart enough to realize that growing up is the biggest adventure of all.

Internet Sites

Do you want to know more about subjects related to this book? Or are you interested in learning about other topics? Then check out FactHound, a fun, easy way to find Internet sites.

Our investigative staff has already sniffed out great sites for you!

Here's how to use FactHound:

1. Visit *www.facthound.com*

2. Select your grade level.

3. To learn more about subjects related to this book, type in the book's ISBN number: **9781434211996**.

4. Click the **Fetch It** button.

FactHound will fetch the best Internet sites for you!